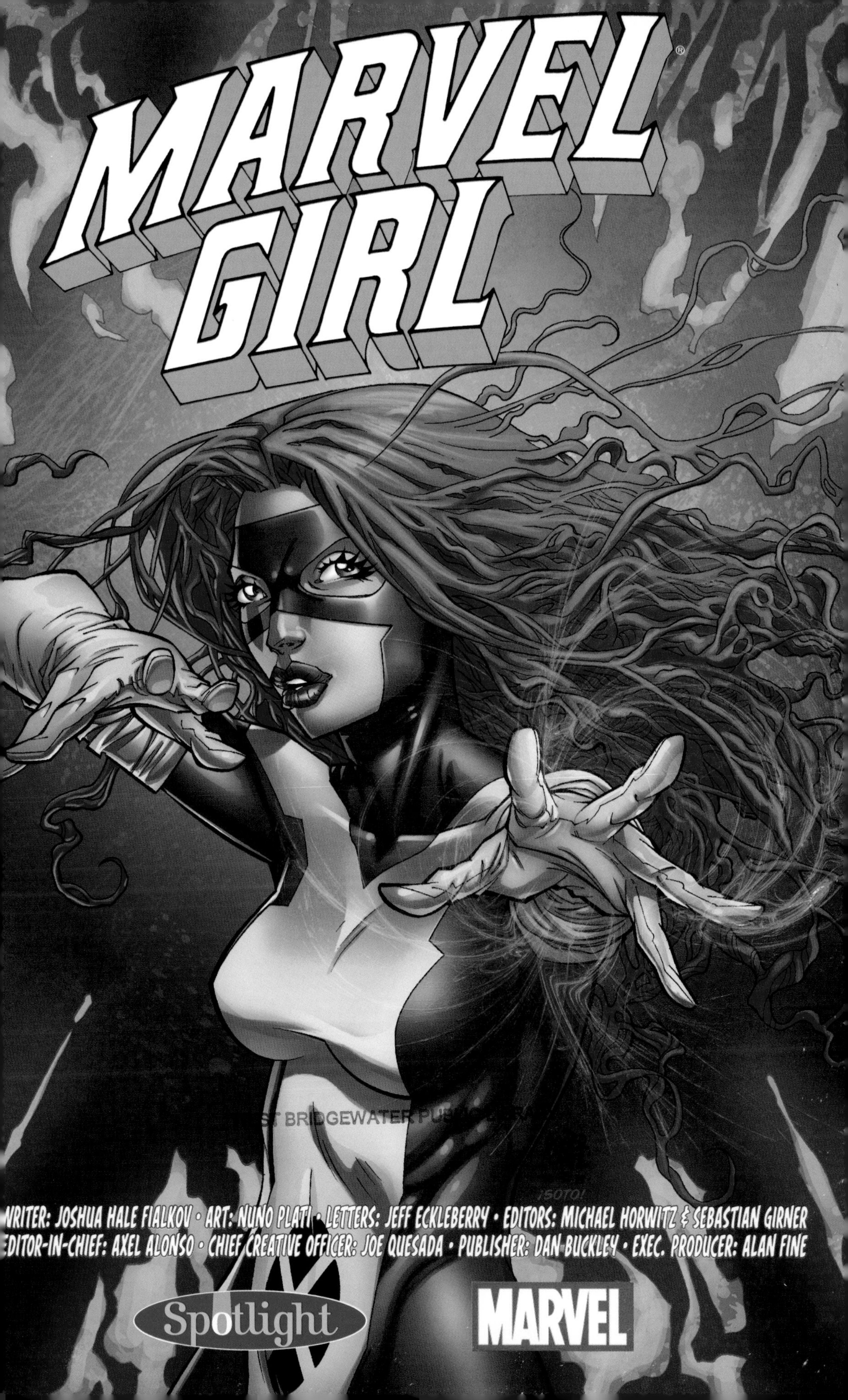
MARVEL GIRL
¡SOTO!
WRITER: JOSHUA HALE FIALKOV • ART: NUNO PLATI • LETTERS: JEFF ECKLEBERRY • EDITORS: MICHAEL HORWITZ & SEBASTIAN GIRNER
EDITOR-IN-CHIEF: AXEL ALONSO • CHIEF CREATIVE OFFICER: JOE QUESADA • PUBLISHER: DAN BUCKLEY • EXEC. PRODUCER: ALAN FINE
Spotlight
MARVEL

visit us at www.abdopublishing.com

Reinforced library bound edition published in 2012 by Spotlight, a division of the ABDO Group, 8000 West 78th Street, Edina, Minnesota 55439. Spotlight produces high-quality reinforced library bound editions for schools and libraries. Published by agreement with Marvel Entertainment, LLC. The stories, characters, and incidents mentioned are entirely fictional. All rights reserved. Used under authorization.

Printed in the United States of America, Melrose Park, Illinois.
052011
092011
♻ This book contains at least 10% recycled materials.

Library of Congress Cataloging-in-Publication Data

Fialkov, Joshua Hale, 1979-
  Marvel girl / writer, Joshua Hale Fialkov ; art, Nuno Plati.
     p. cm. -- (X-men: first class)
  ISBN 978-1-59961-950-7
  1. Graphic novels. I. Plati, Nuno. II. Title.
  PN6728.X2F48 2011
  741.5'973--dc22
                                2011013934

All Spotlight books are reinforced library bindings
and manufactured in the United States of America.

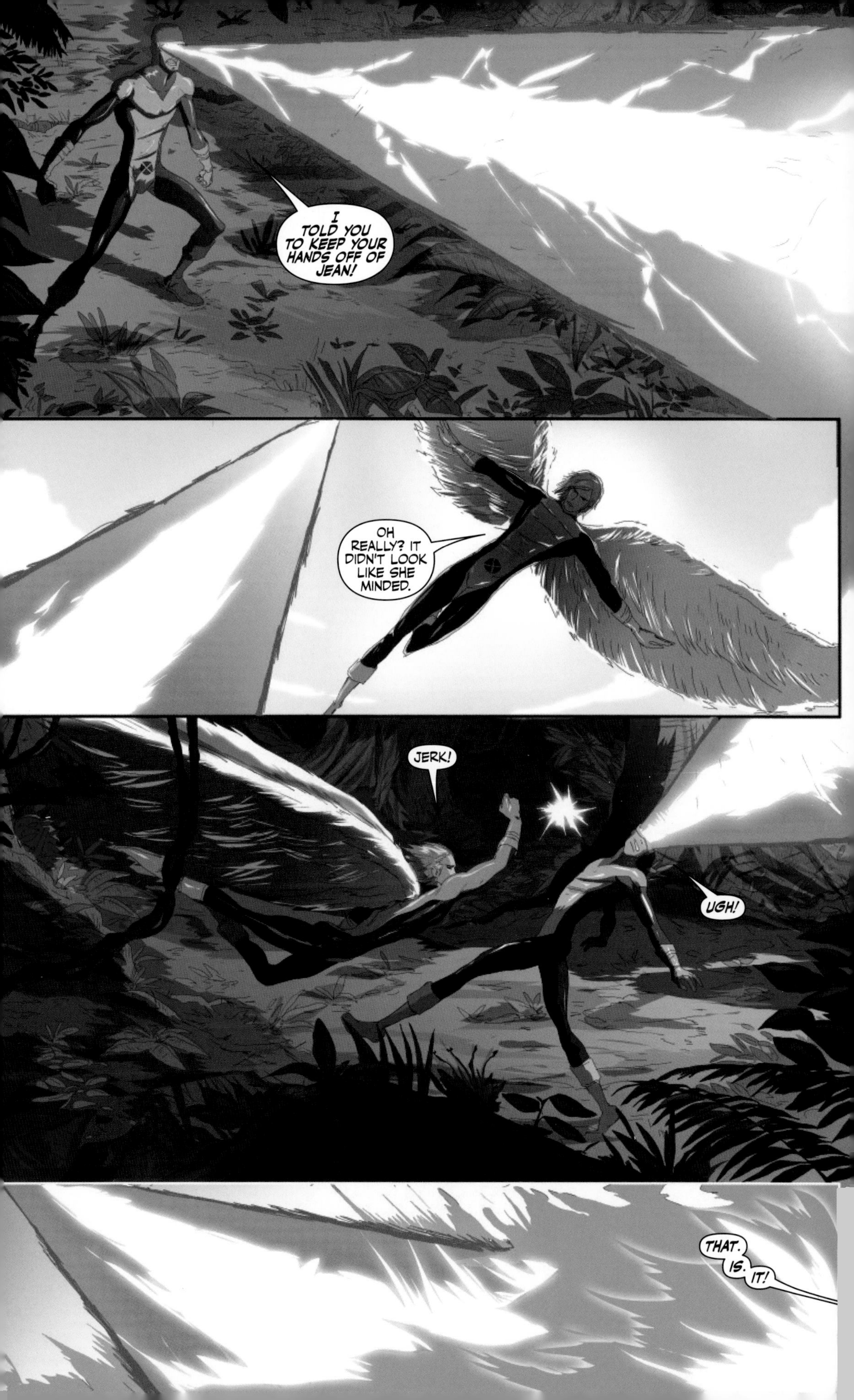
I TOLD YOU TO KEEP YOUR HANDS OFF OF JEAN!
OH REALLY? IT DIDN'T LOOK LIKE SHE MINDED.
JERK!
UGH!
THAT. IS. IT!

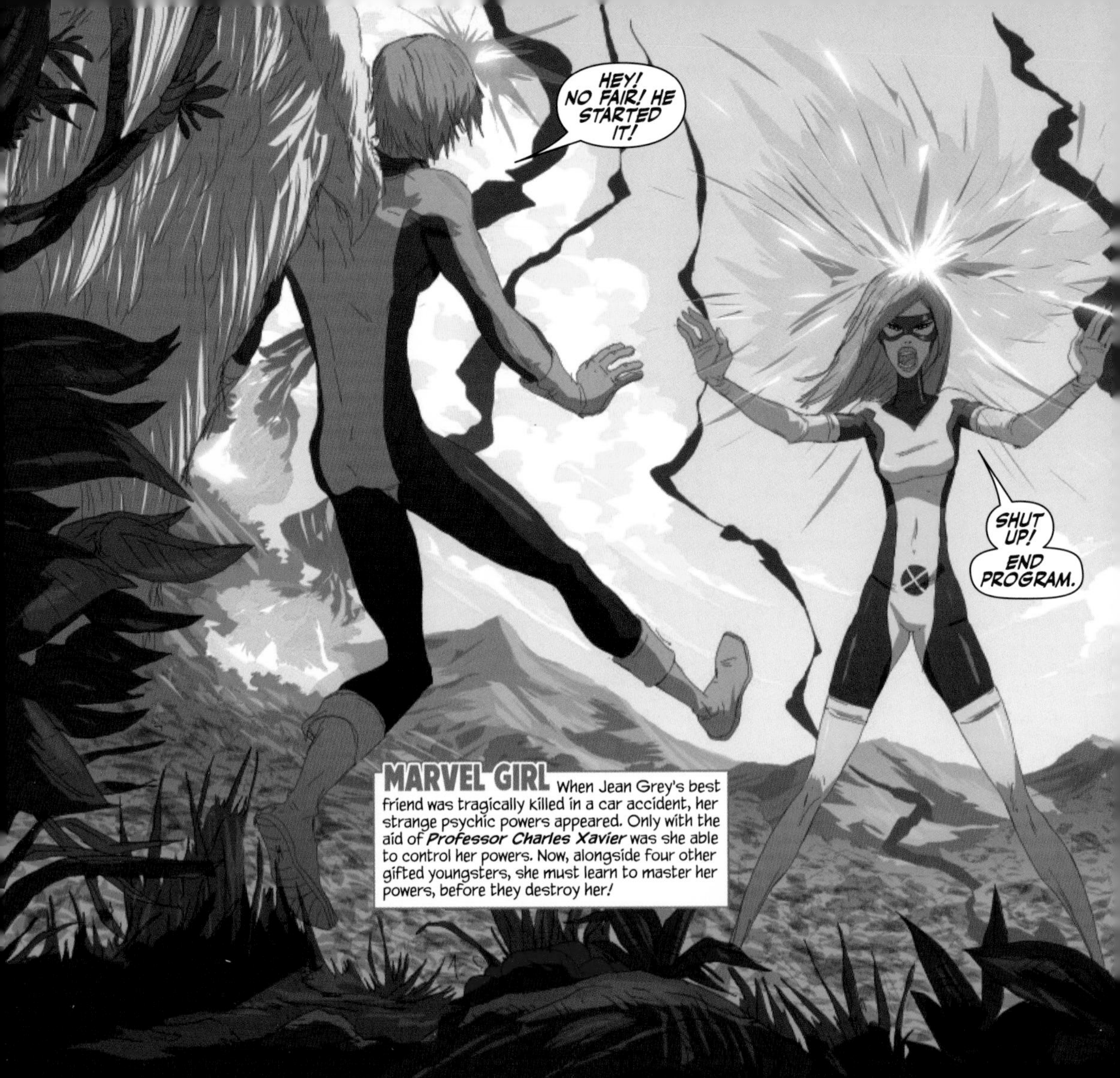
HEY! NO FAIR! HE STARTED IT!
SHUT UP! END PROGRAM.
MARVEL GIRL When Jean Grey's best friend was tragically killed in a car accident, her strange psychic powers appeared. Only with the aid of Professor Charles Xavier was she able to control her powers. Now, alongside four other gifted youngsters, she must learn to master her powers, before they destroy her!
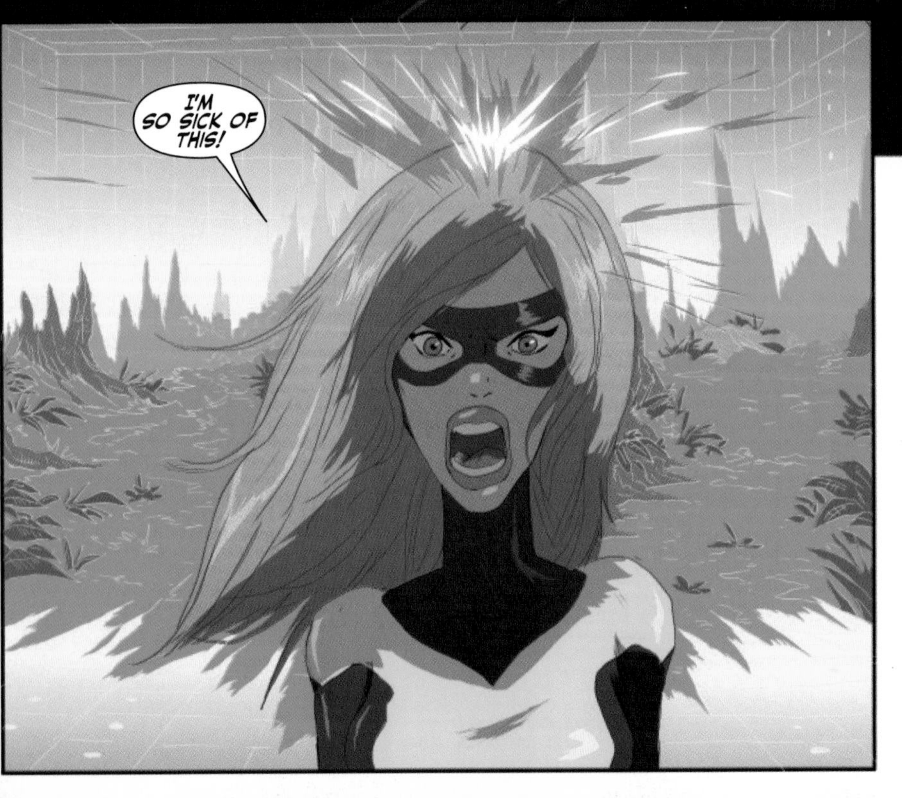
I'M SO SICK OF THIS!
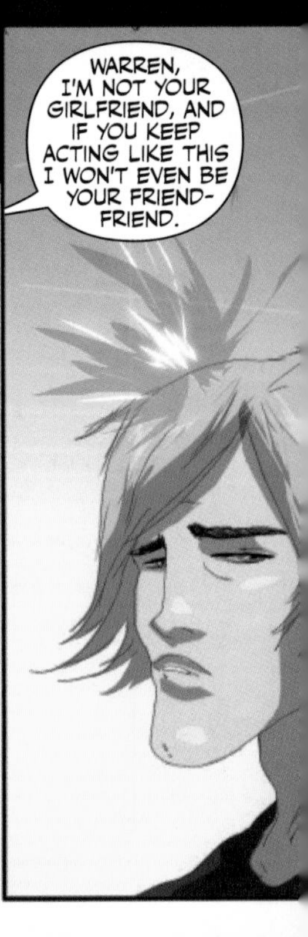
WARREN, I'M NOT YOUR GIRLFRIEND, AND IF YOU KEEP ACTING LIKE THIS I WON'T EVEN BE YOUR FRIEND-FRIEND.

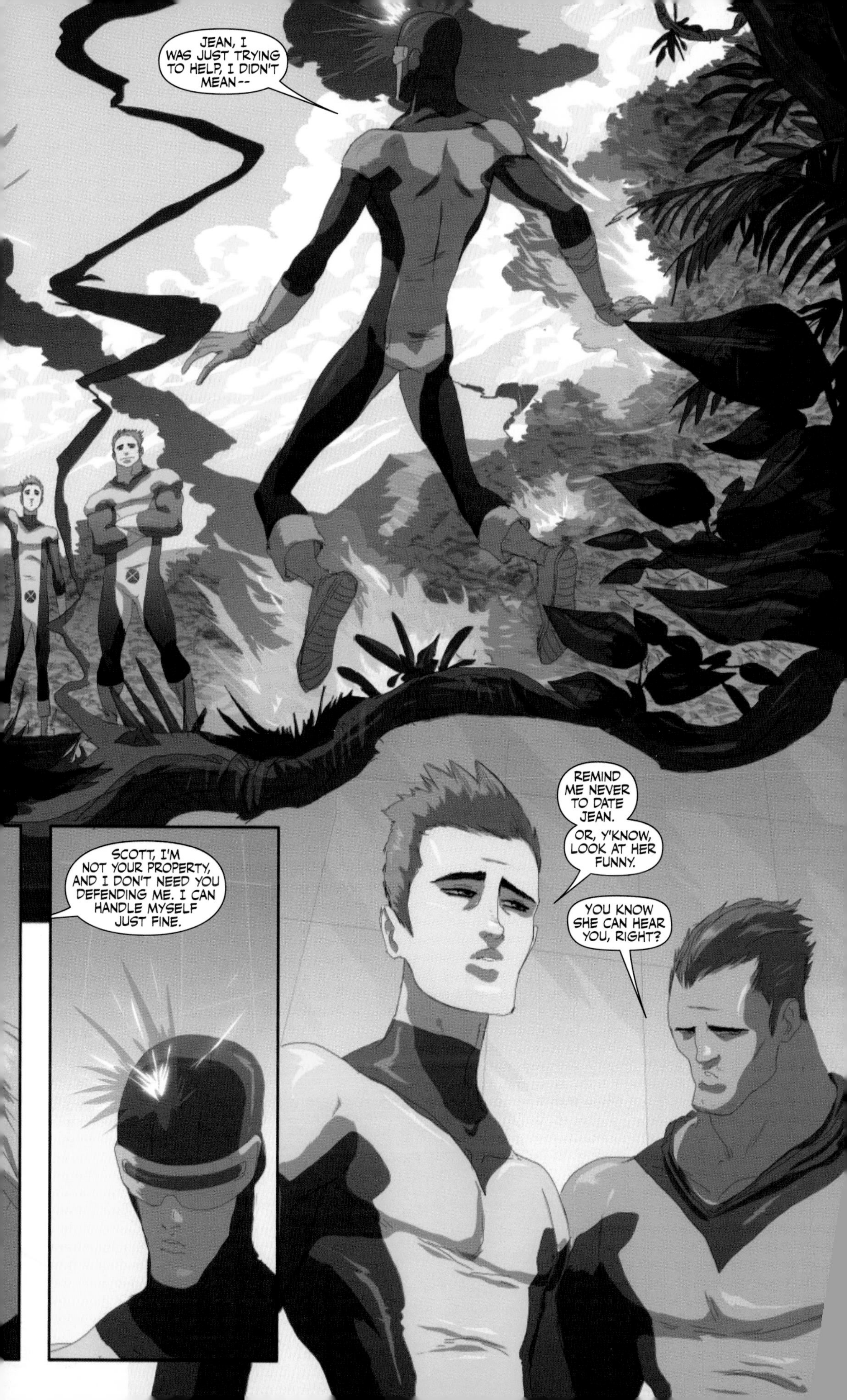
JEAN, I WAS JUST TRYING TO HELP, I DIDN'T MEAN--
SCOTT, I'M NOT YOUR PROPERTY, AND I DON'T NEED YOU DEFENDING ME. I CAN HANDLE MYSELF JUST FINE.
REMIND ME NEVER TO DATE JEAN.
OR, Y'KNOW, LOOK AT HER FUNNY.
YOU KNOW SHE CAN HEAR YOU, RIGHT?

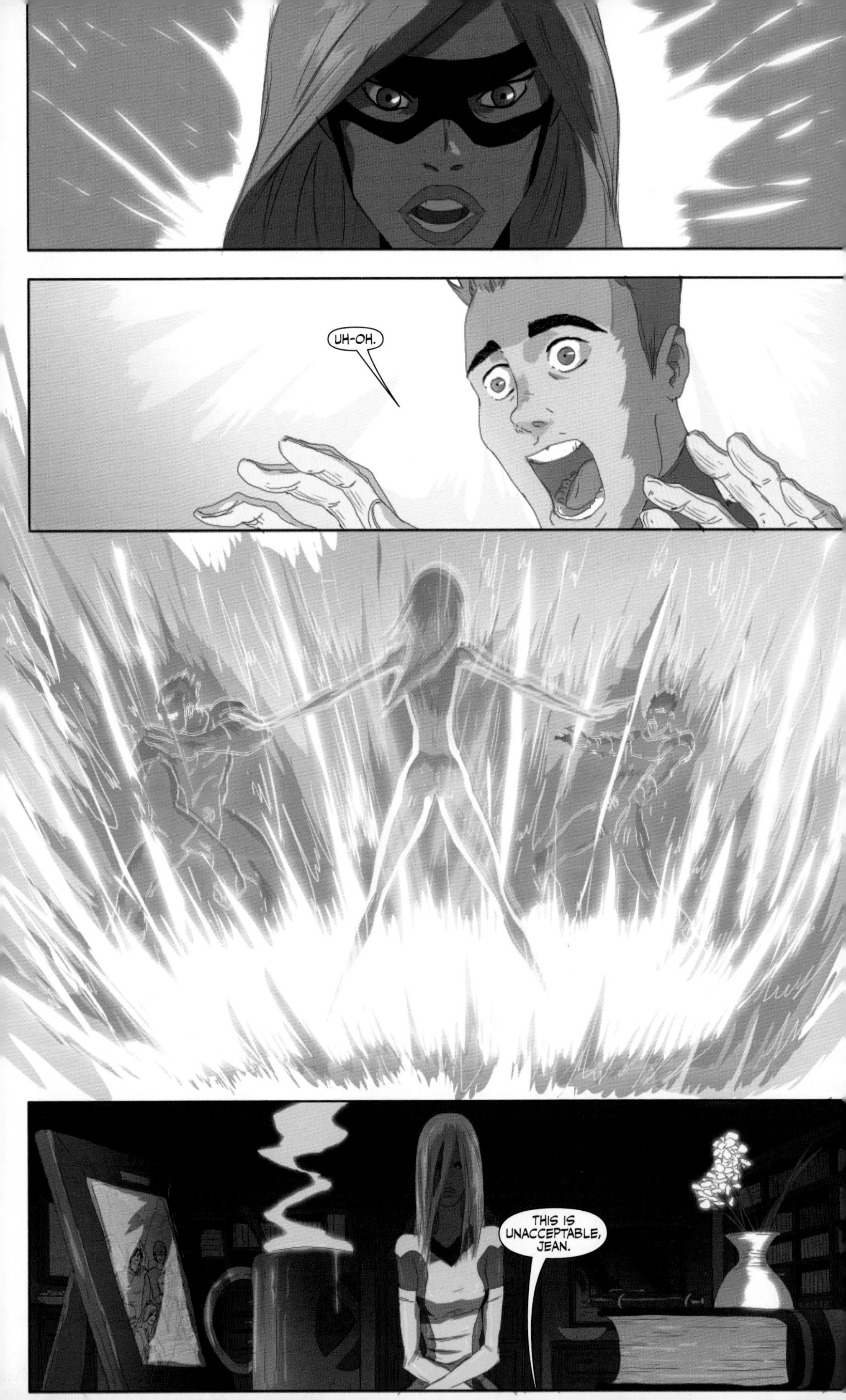
UH-OH.
THIS IS UNACCEPTABLE, JEAN.

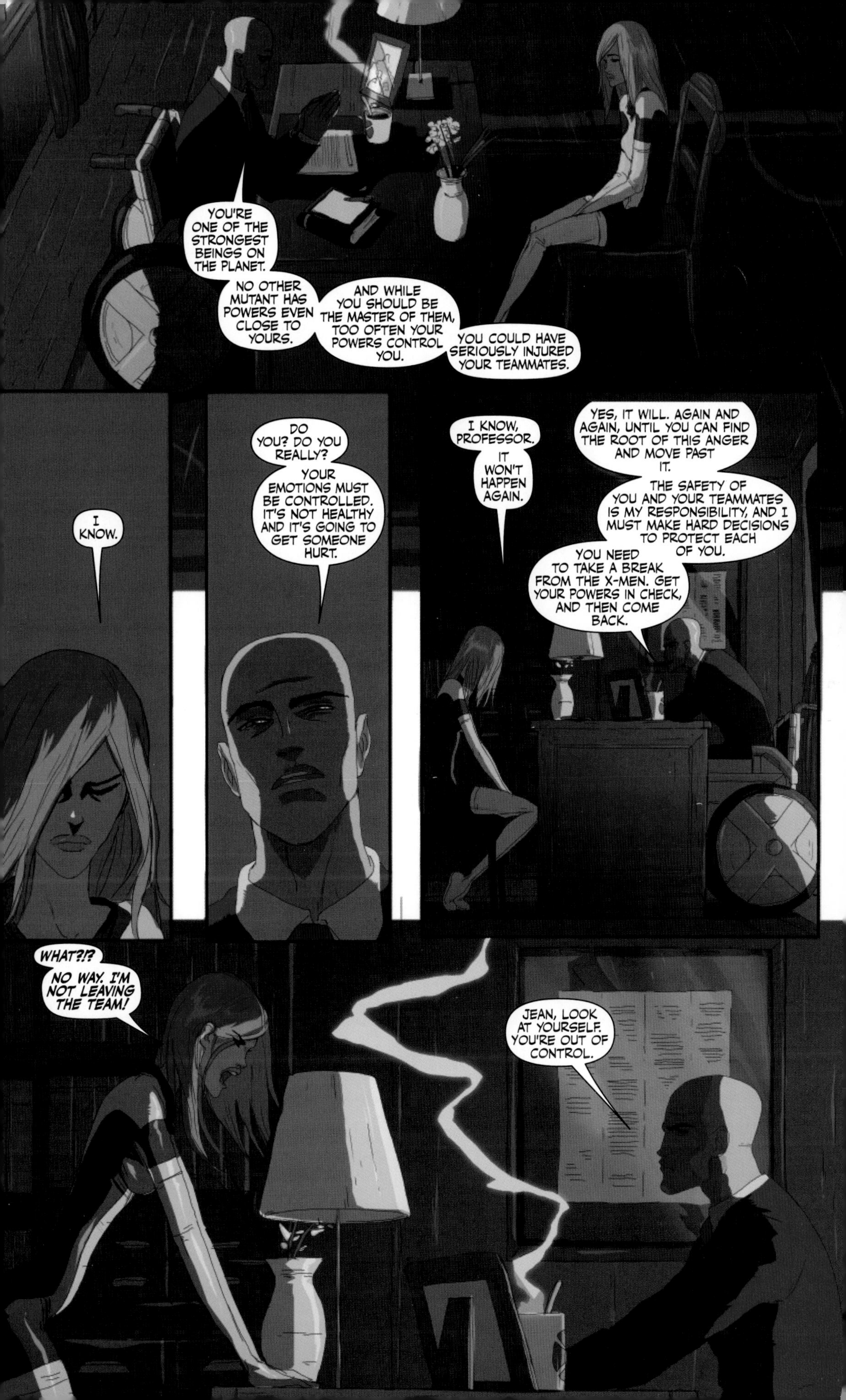
YOU'RE ONE OF THE STRONGEST BEINGS ON THE PLANET.
NO OTHER MUTANT HAS POWERS EVEN CLOSE TO YOURS.
AND WHILE YOU SHOULD BE THE MASTER OF THEM, TOO OFTEN YOUR POWERS CONTROL YOU.
YOU COULD HAVE SERIOUSLY INJURED YOUR TEAMMATES.
I KNOW.
DO YOU? DO YOU REALLY?
YOUR EMOTIONS MUST BE CONTROLLED. IT'S NOT HEALTHY AND IT'S GOING TO GET SOMEONE HURT.
I KNOW, PROFESSOR.
IT WON'T HAPPEN AGAIN.
YES, IT WILL. AGAIN AND AGAIN, UNTIL YOU CAN FIND THE ROOT OF THIS ANGER AND MOVE PAST IT.
THE SAFETY OF YOU AND YOUR TEAMMATES IS MY RESPONSIBILITY, AND I MUST MAKE HARD DECISIONS TO PROTECT EACH OF YOU.
YOU NEED TO TAKE A BREAK FROM THE X-MEN. GET YOUR POWERS IN CHECK, AND THEN COME BACK.
WHAT?!?
NO WAY. I'M NOT LEAVING THE TEAM!
JEAN, LOOK AT YOURSELF. YOU'RE OUT OF CONTROL.

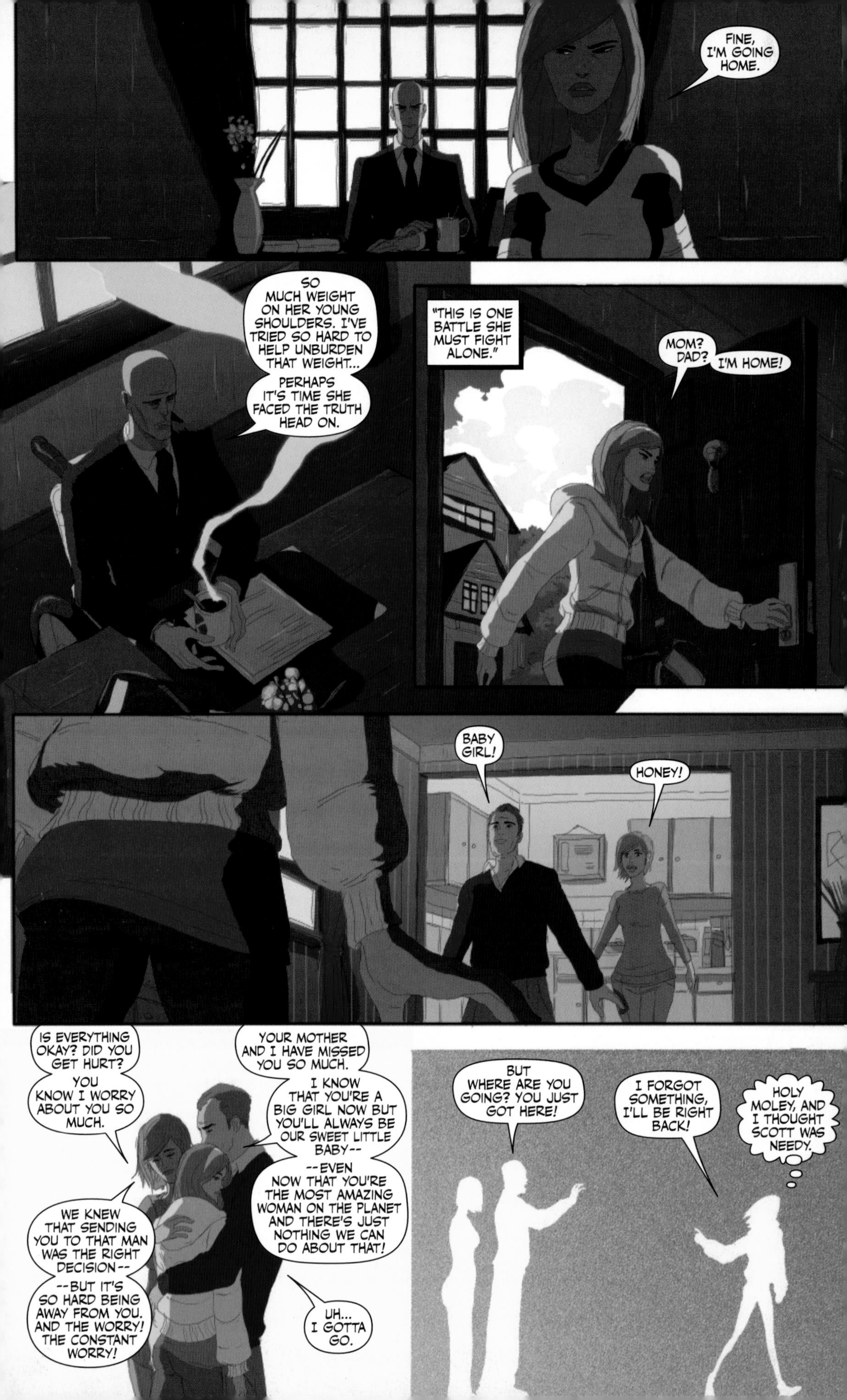
FINE, I'M GOING HOME.
SO MUCH WEIGHT ON HER YOUNG SHOULDERS. I'VE TRIED SO HARD TO HELP UNBURDEN THAT WEIGHT...
PERHAPS IT'S TIME SHE FACED THE TRUTH HEAD ON.
"THIS IS ONE BATTLE SHE MUST FIGHT ALONE."
MOM? DAD?
I'M HOME!
BABY GIRL!
HONEY!
IS EVERYTHING OKAY? DID YOU GET HURT?
YOU KNOW I WORRY ABOUT YOU SO MUCH.
YOUR MOTHER AND I HAVE MISSED YOU SO MUCH.
I KNOW THAT YOU'RE A BIG GIRL NOW BUT YOU'LL ALWAYS BE OUR SWEET LITTLE BABY--
--EVEN NOW THAT YOU'RE THE MOST AMAZING WOMAN ON THE PLANET AND THERE'S JUST NOTHING WE CAN DO ABOUT THAT!
WE KNEW THAT SENDING YOU TO THAT MAN WAS THE RIGHT DECISION--
--BUT IT'S SO HARD BEING AWAY FROM YOU. AND THE WORRY! THE CONSTANT WORRY!
UH... I GOTTA GO.
BUT WHERE ARE YOU GOING? YOU JUST GOT HERE!
I FORGOT SOMETHING, I'LL BE RIGHT BACK!
HOLY MOLEY, AND I THOUGHT SCOTT WAS NEEDY.

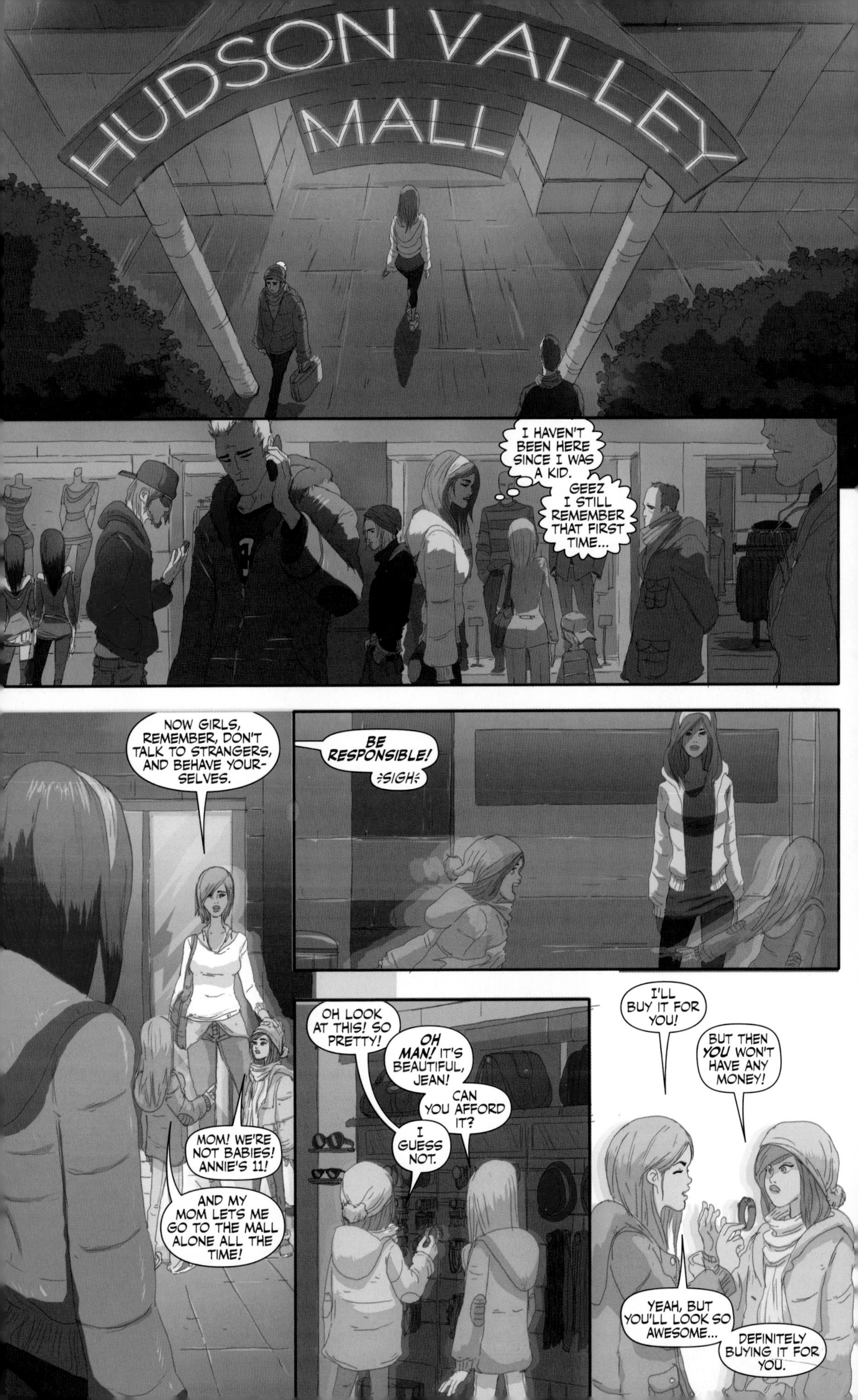
HUDSON VALLEY MALL
I HAVEN'T BEEN HERE SINCE I WAS A KID.
GEEZ I STILL REMEMBER THAT FIRST TIME...
NOW GIRLS, REMEMBER, DON'T TALK TO STRANGERS, AND BEHAVE YOUR-SELVES.
BE RESPONSIBLE!
SIGH
MOM! WE'RE NOT BABIES! ANNIE'S 11!
AND MY MOM LETS ME GO TO THE MALL ALONE ALL THE TIME!
OH LOOK AT THIS! SO PRETTY!
OH MAN! IT'S BEAUTIFUL, JEAN!
CAN YOU AFFORD IT?
I GUESS NOT.
I'LL BUY IT FOR YOU!
BUT THEN YOU WON'T HAVE ANY MONEY!
YEAH, BUT YOU'LL LOOK SO AWESOME...
DEFINITELY BUYING IT FOR YOU.

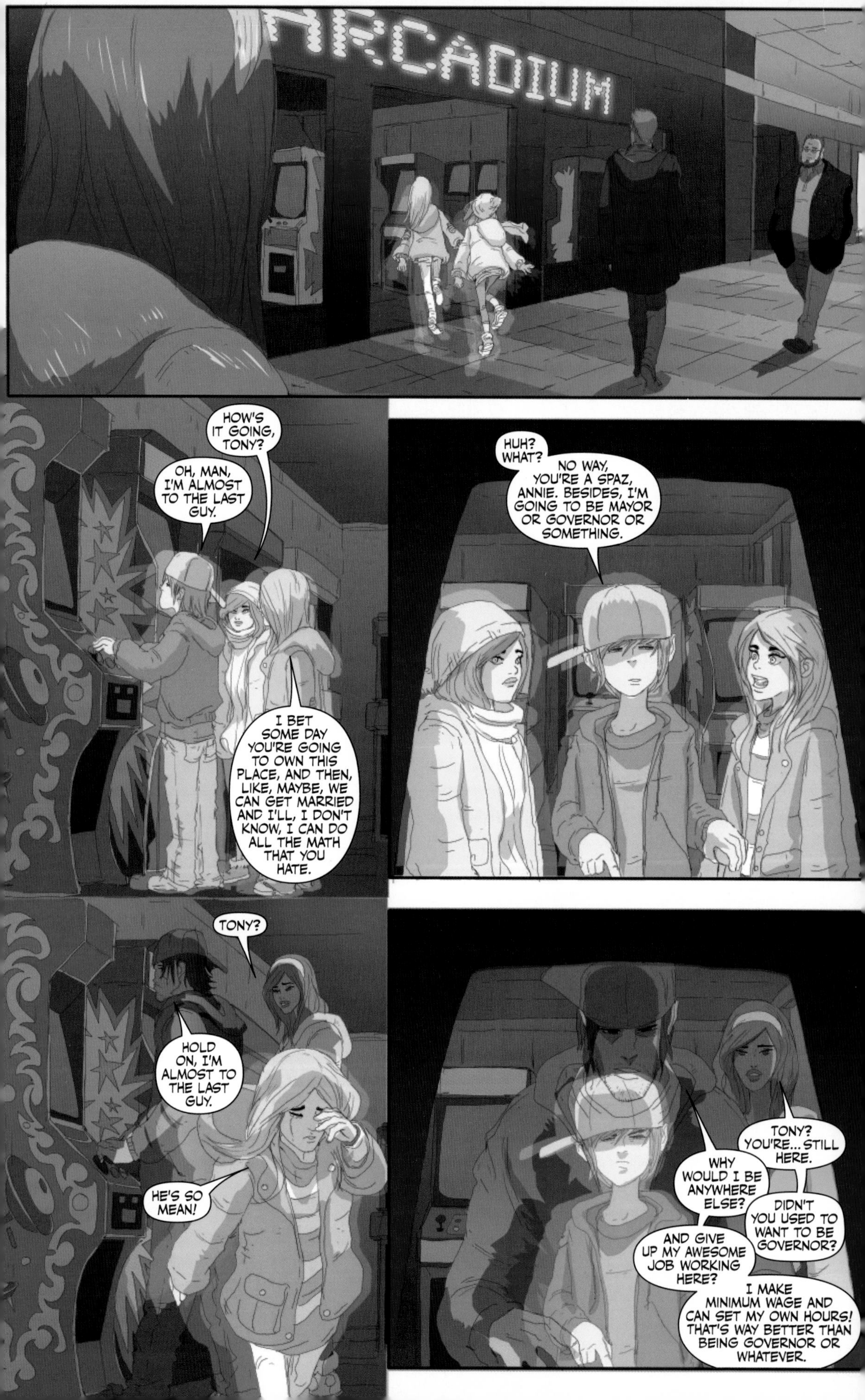
ARCADIUM
HOW'S IT GOING, TONY?
OH, MAN, I'M ALMOST TO THE LAST GUY.
I BET SOME DAY YOU'RE GOING TO OWN THIS PLACE, AND THEN, LIKE, MAYBE, WE CAN GET MARRIED AND I'LL, I DON'T KNOW, I CAN DO ALL THE MATH THAT YOU HATE.
HUH? WHAT?
NO WAY, YOU'RE A SPAZ, ANNIE. BESIDES, I'M GOING TO BE MAYOR OR GOVERNOR OR SOMETHING.
TONY?
HOLD ON, I'M ALMOST TO THE LAST GUY.
HE'S SO MEAN!
TONY? YOU'RE... STILL HERE.
WHY WOULD I BE ANYWHERE ELSE?
DIDN'T YOU USED TO WANT TO BE GOVERNOR?
AND GIVE UP MY AWESOME JOB WORKING HERE?
I MAKE MINIMUM WAGE AND CAN SET MY OWN HOURS! THAT'S WAY BETTER THAN BEING GOVERNOR OR WHATEVER.

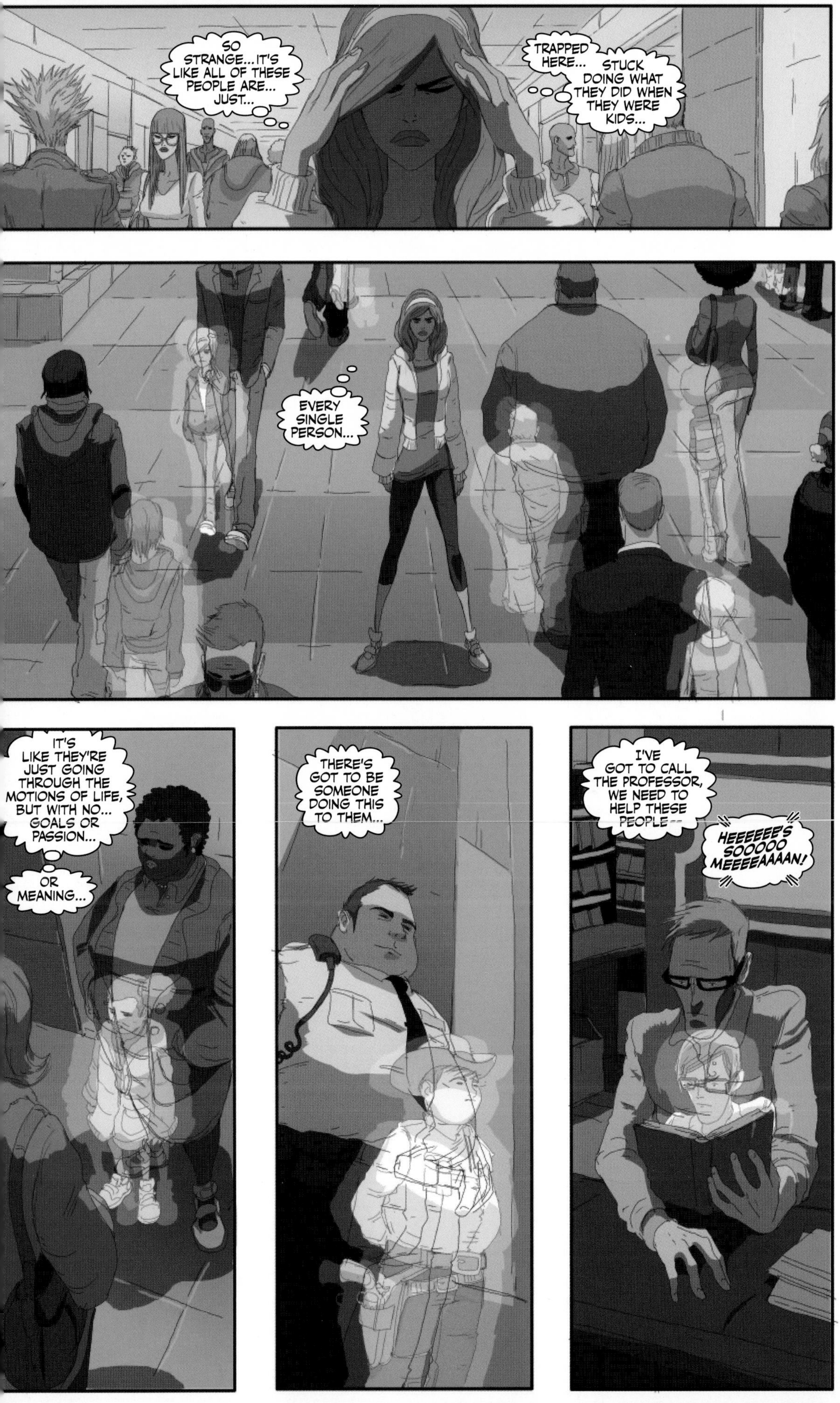
SO STRANGE...IT'S LIKE ALL OF THESE PEOPLE ARE... JUST...
TRAPPED HERE...
STUCK DOING WHAT THEY DID WHEN THEY WERE KIDS...
EVERY SINGLE PERSON...
IT'S LIKE THEY'RE JUST GOING THROUGH THE MOTIONS OF LIFE, BUT WITH NO... GOALS OR PASSION...
OR MEANING...
THERE'S GOT TO BE SOMEONE DOING THIS TO THEM...
I'VE GOT TO CALL THE PROFESSOR, WE NEED TO HELP THESE PEOPLE--
HEEEEEE'S SOOOOO MEEEEAAAAN!

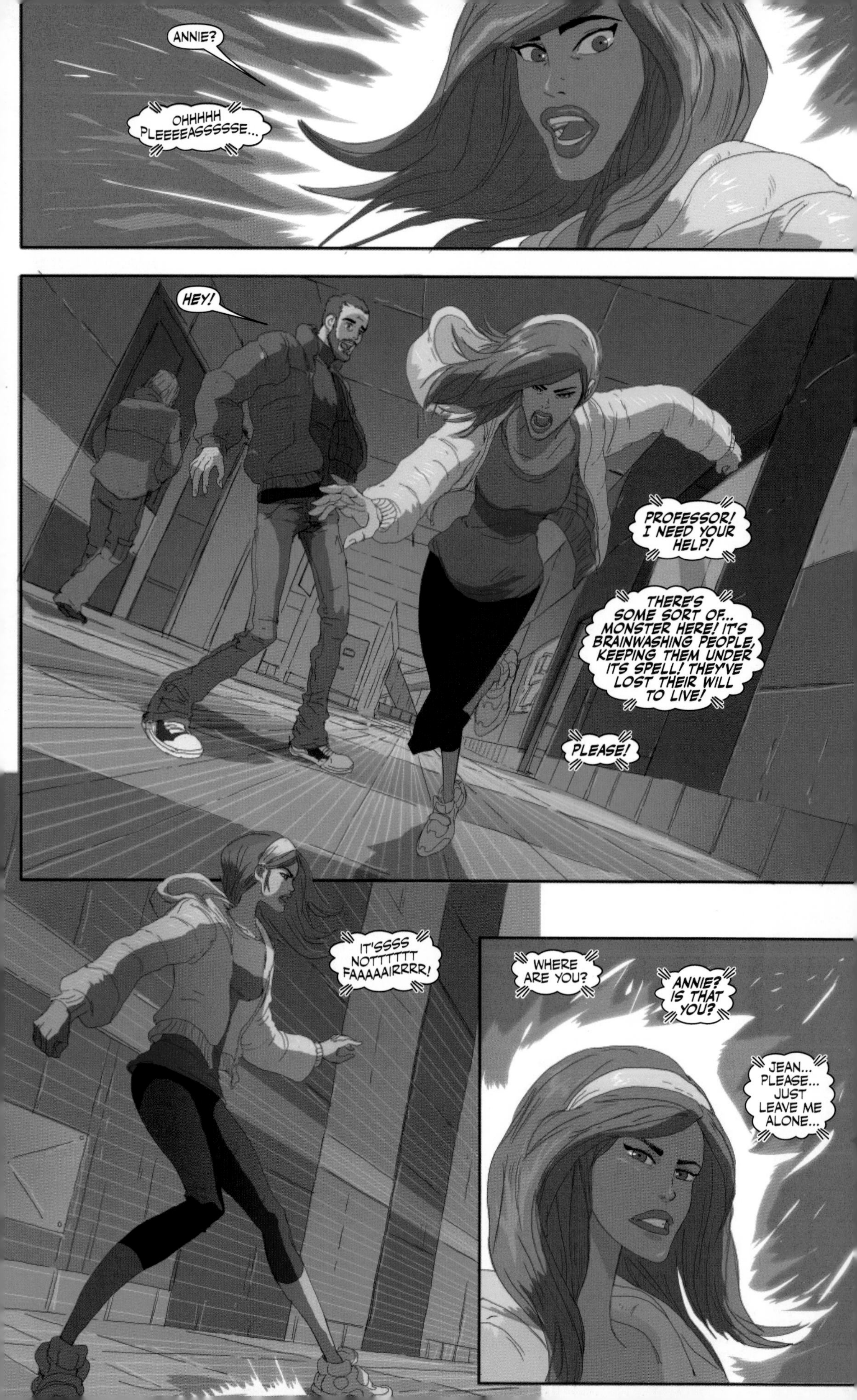
ANNIE?
OHHHHH PLEEEEASSSSSE...
HEY!
PROFESSOR! I NEED YOUR HELP!
THERE'S SOME SORT OF... MONSTER HERE! IT'S BRAINWASHING PEOPLE, KEEPING THEM UNDER ITS SPELL! THEY'VE LOST THEIR WILL TO LIVE!
PLEASE!
IT'SSSS NOTTTTTT FAAAAAIRRRR!
WHERE ARE YOU?
ANNIE? IS THAT YOU?
JEAN... PLEASE... JUST LEAVE ME ALONE...

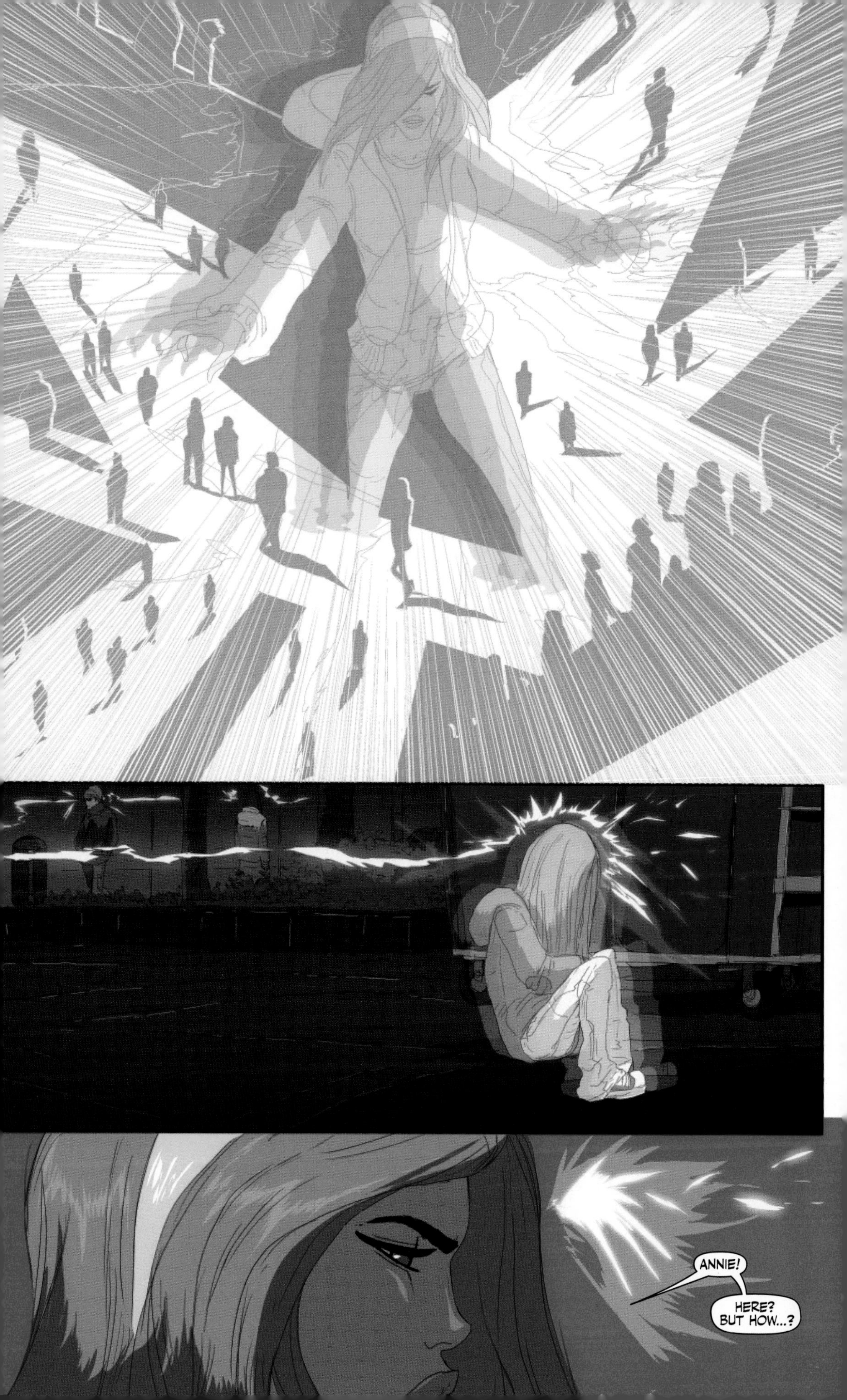
ANNIE!
HERE? BUT HOW...?

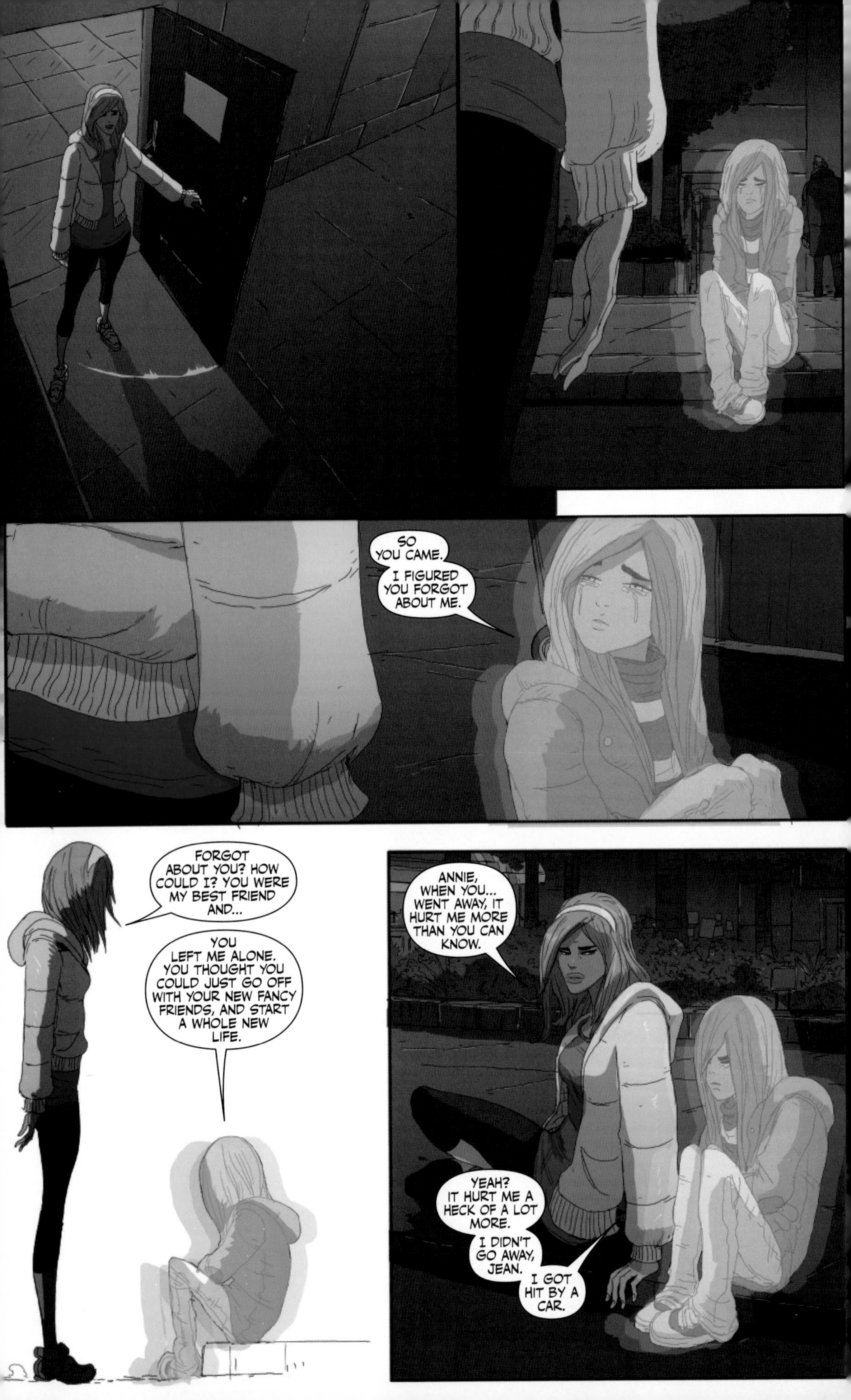
SO YOU CAME. I FIGURED YOU FORGOT ABOUT ME.
FORGOT ABOUT YOU? HOW COULD I? YOU WERE MY BEST FRIEND AND...
YOU LEFT ME ALONE. YOU THOUGHT YOU COULD JUST GO OFF WITH YOUR NEW FANCY FRIENDS, AND START A WHOLE NEW LIFE.
ANNIE, WHEN YOU... WENT AWAY, IT HURT ME MORE THAN YOU CAN KNOW.
YEAH? IT HURT ME A HECK OF A LOT MORE.
I DIDN'T GO AWAY, JEAN.
I GOT HIT BY A CAR.

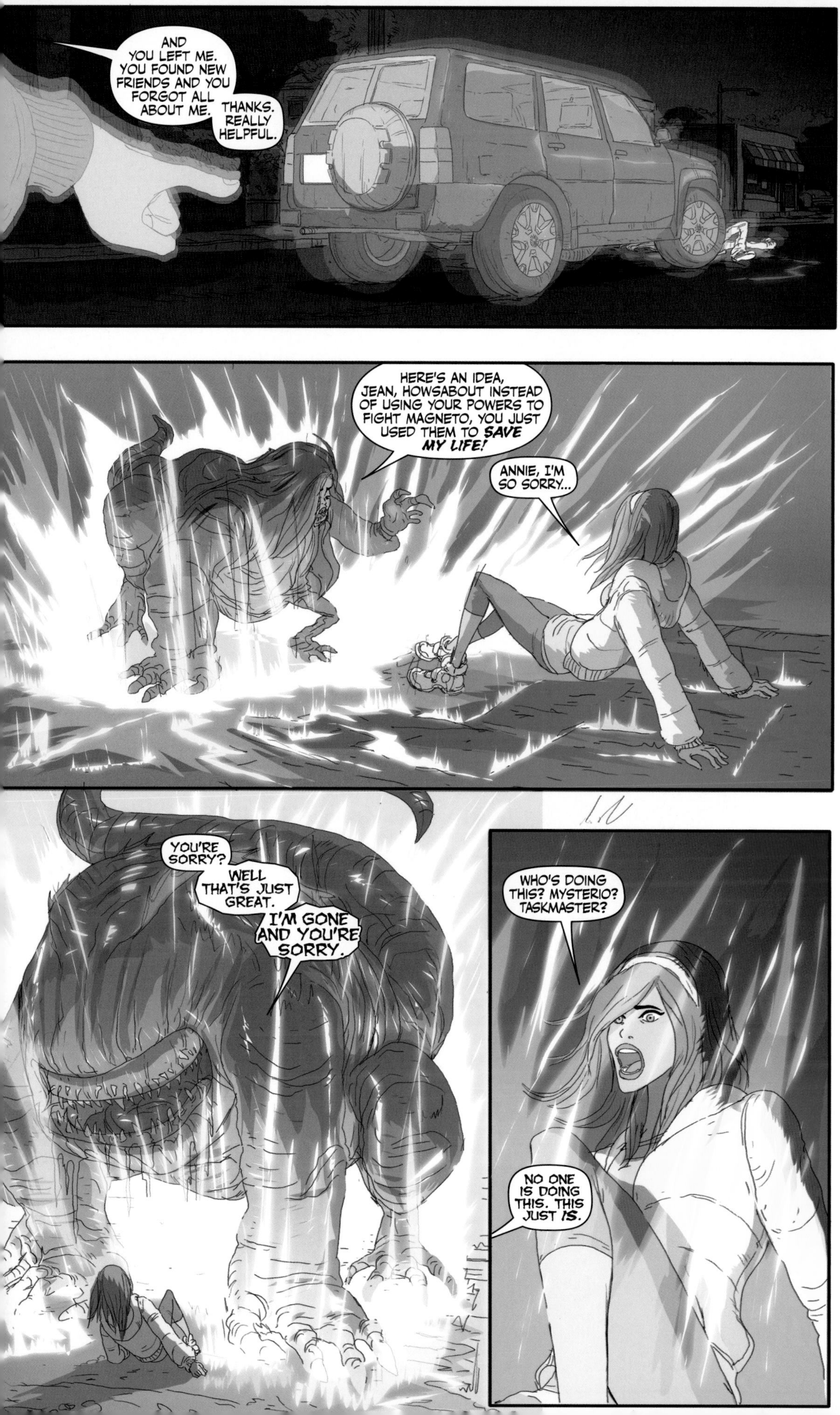
AND YOU LEFT ME. YOU FOUND NEW FRIENDS AND YOU FORGOT ALL ABOUT ME.
THANKS. REALLY HELPFUL.
HERE'S AN IDEA, JEAN, HOWSABOUT INSTEAD OF USING YOUR POWERS TO FIGHT MAGNETO, YOU JUST USED THEM TO SAVE MY LIFE!
ANNIE, I'M SO SORRY...
YOU'RE SORRY?
WELL THAT'S JUST GREAT.
I'M GONE AND YOU'RE SORRY.
WHO'S DOING THIS? MYSTERIO? TASKMASTER?
NO ONE IS DOING THIS. THIS JUST IS.

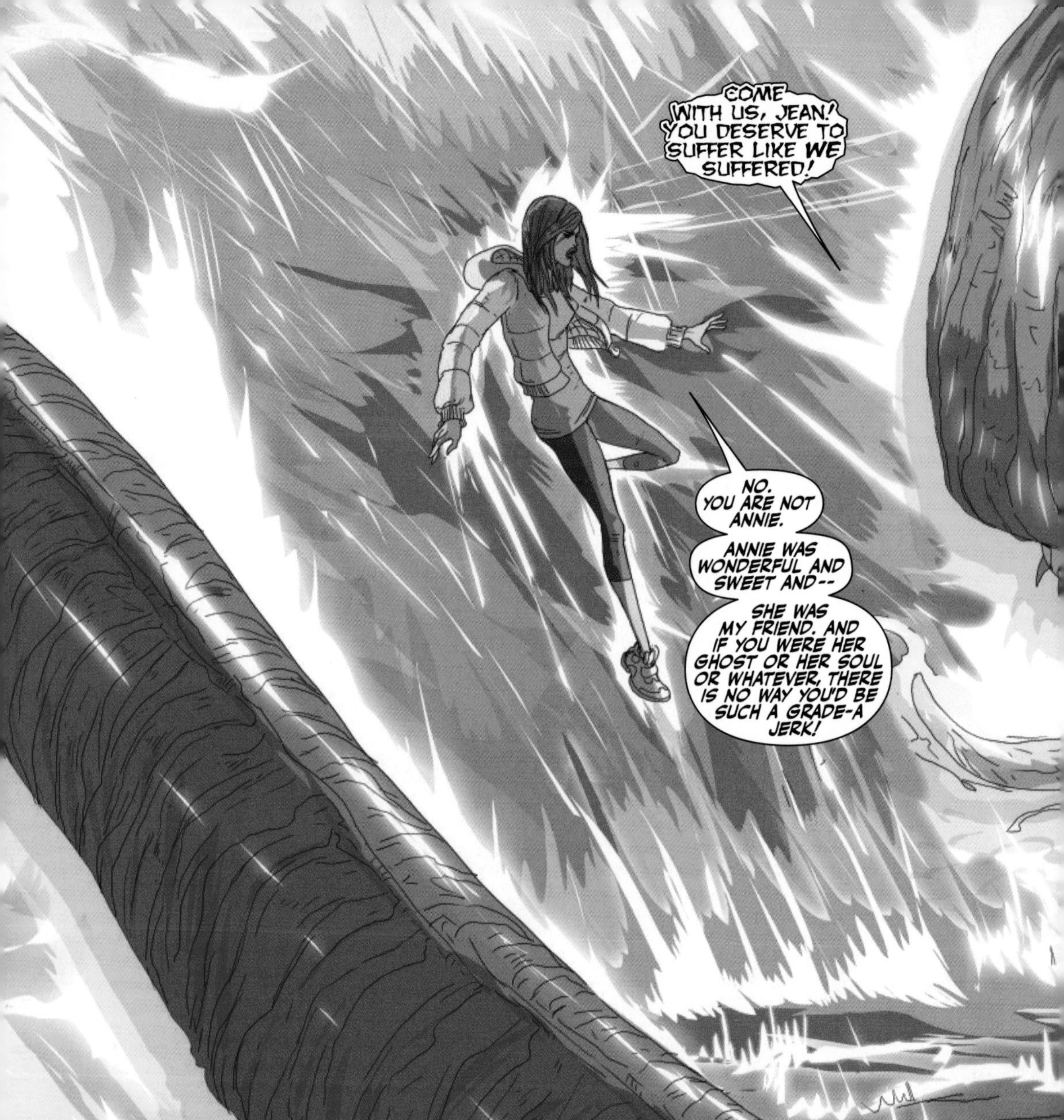
COME WITH US, JEAN! YOU DESERVE TO SUFFER LIKE WE SUFFERED!
NO. YOU ARE NOT ANNIE.
ANNIE WAS WONDERFUL AND SWEET AND--
SHE WAS MY FRIEND. AND IF YOU WERE HER GHOST OR HER SOUL OR WHATEVER, THERE IS NO WAY YOU'D BE SUCH A GRADE-A JERK!

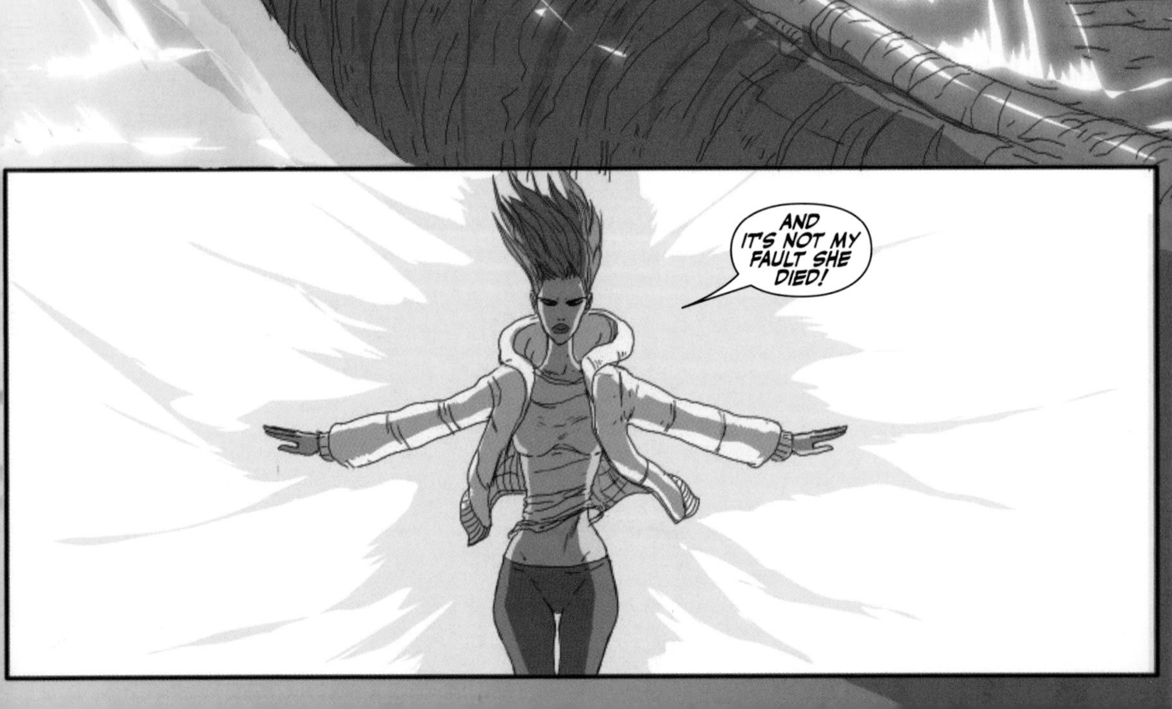
AND IT'S NOT MY FAULT SHE DIED!

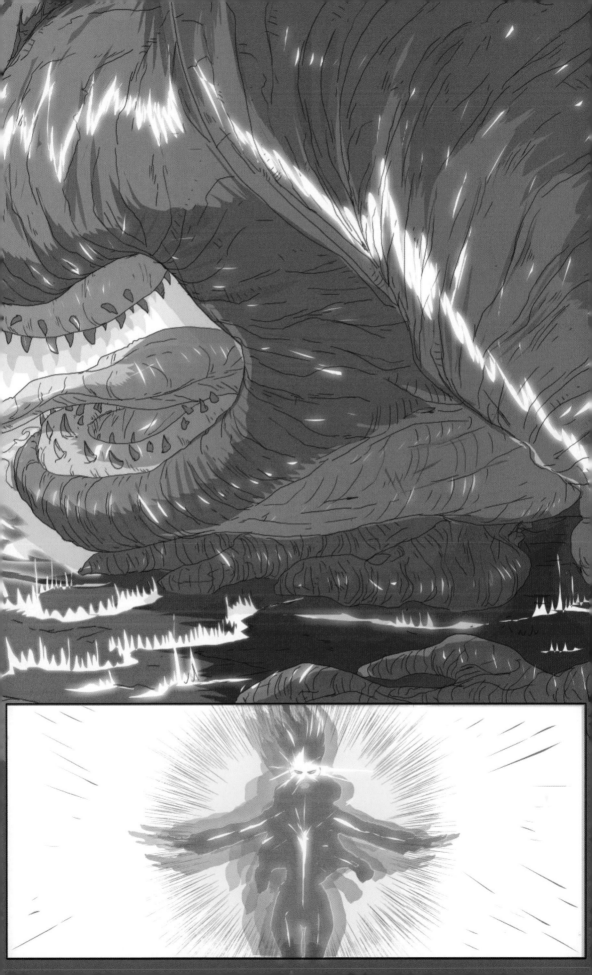

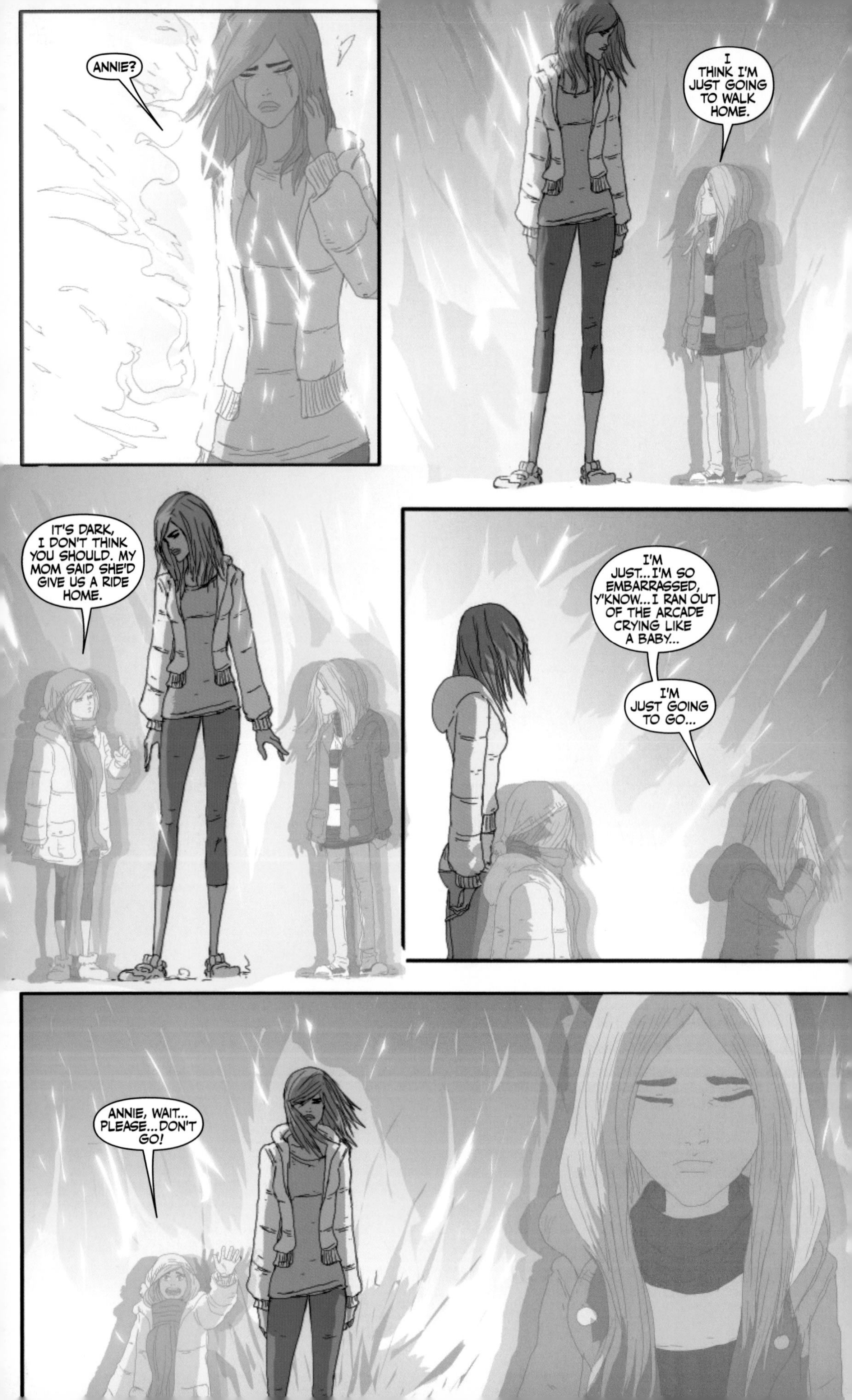
ANNIE?
I THINK I'M JUST GOING TO WALK HOME.
IT'S DARK, I DON'T THINK YOU SHOULD. MY MOM SAID SHE'D GIVE US A RIDE HOME.
I'M JUST...I'M SO EMBARRASSED, Y'KNOW...I RAN OUT OF THE ARCADE CRYING LIKE A BABY...
I'M JUST GOING TO GO...
ANNIE, WAIT... PLEASE...DON'T GO!

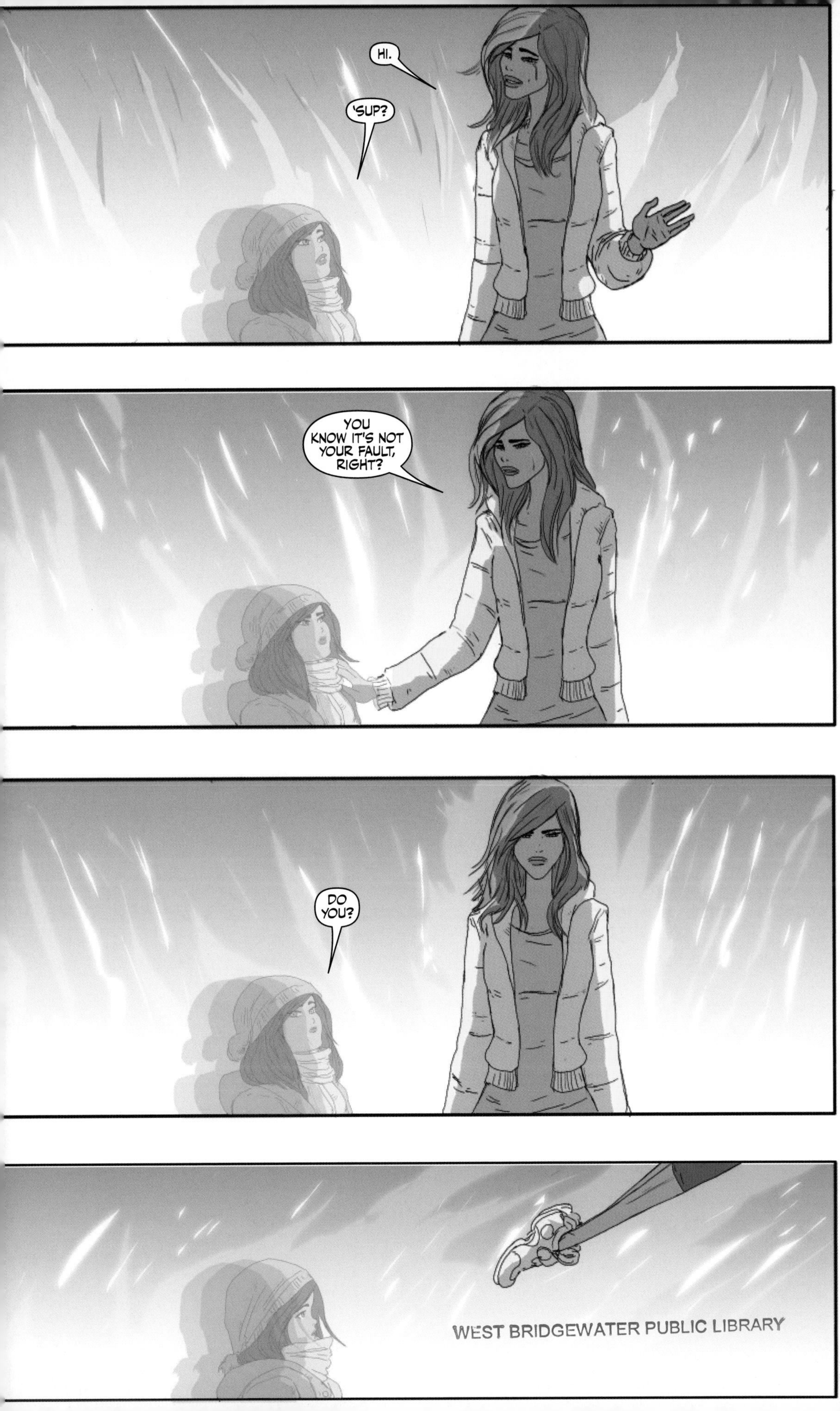
HI.
'SUP?
YOU KNOW IT'S NOT YOUR FAULT, RIGHT?
DO YOU?

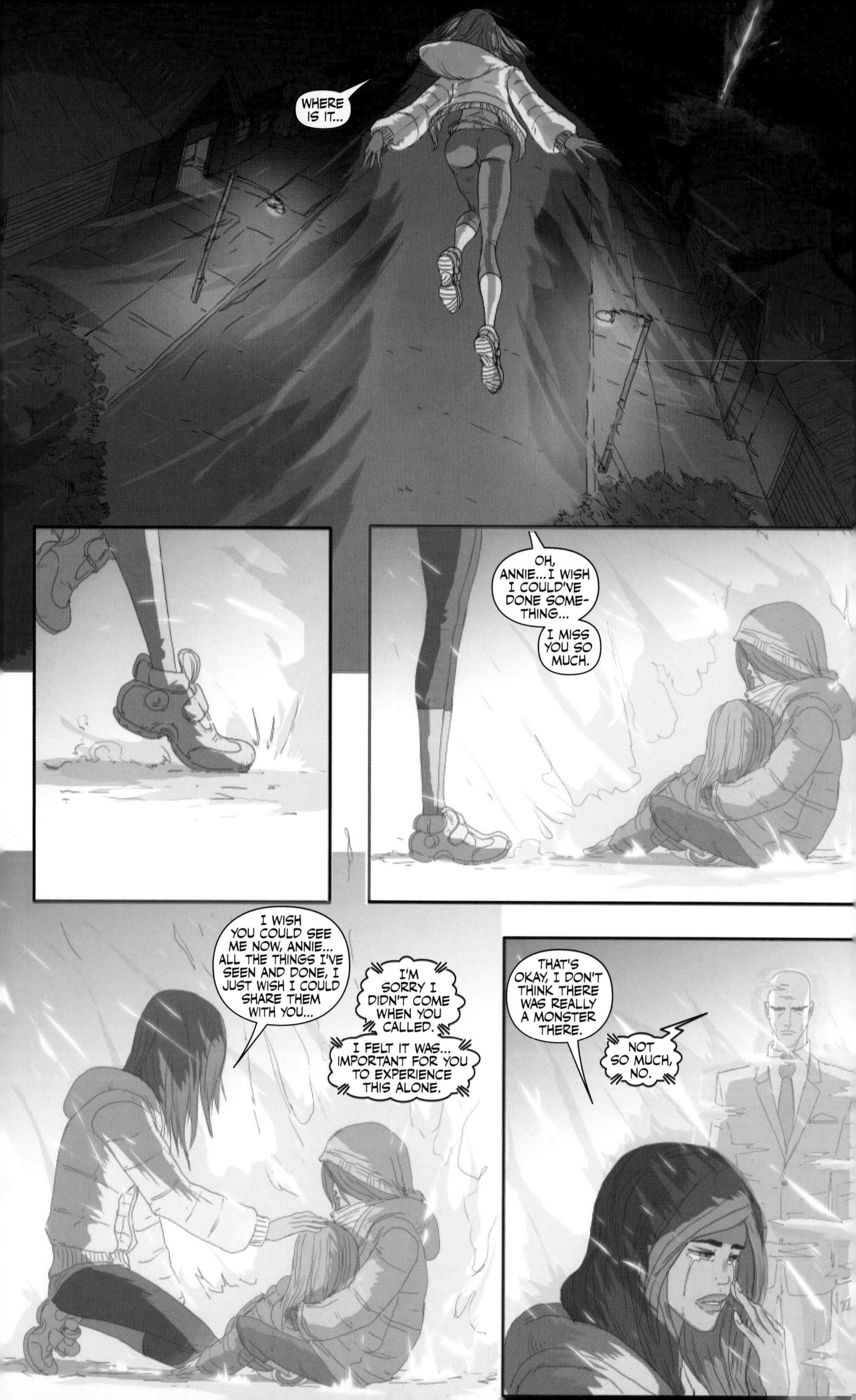
WHERE IS IT...
OH, ANNIE...I WISH I COULD'VE DONE SOME-THING...
I MISS YOU SO MUCH.
I WISH YOU COULD SEE ME NOW, ANNIE... ALL THE THINGS I'VE SEEN AND DONE, I JUST WISH I COULD SHARE THEM WITH YOU...
I'M SORRY I DIDN'T COME WHEN YOU CALLED.
I FELT IT WAS... IMPORTANT FOR YOU TO EXPERIENCE THIS ALONE.
THAT'S OKAY, I DON'T THINK THERE WAS REALLY A MONSTER THERE.
NOT SO MUCH, NO.

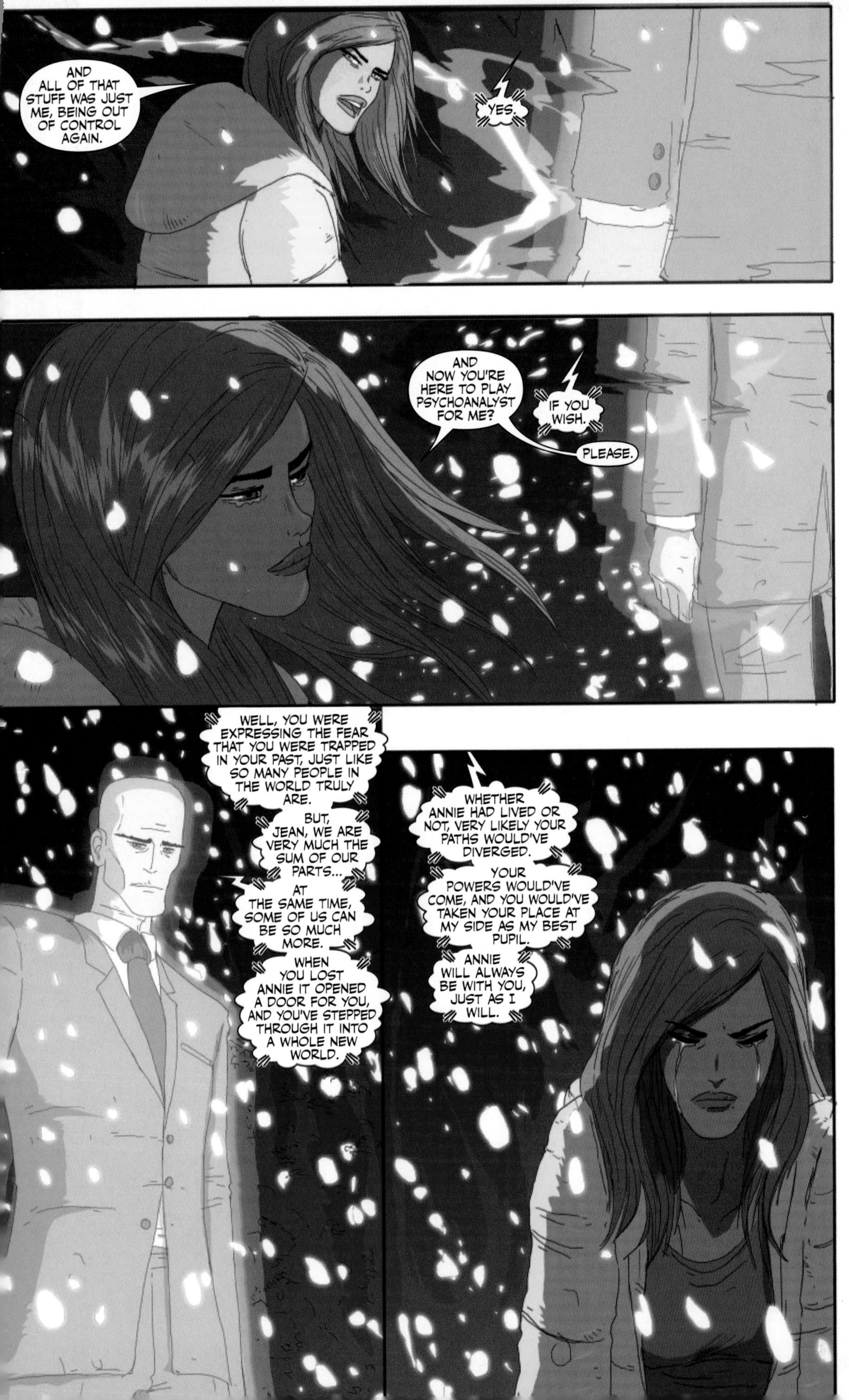
AND ALL OF THAT STUFF WAS JUST ME, BEING OUT OF CONTROL AGAIN.
YES.
AND NOW YOU'RE HERE TO PLAY PSYCHOANALYST FOR ME?
IF YOU WISH.
PLEASE.
WELL, YOU WERE EXPRESSING THE FEAR THAT YOU WERE TRAPPED IN YOUR PAST, JUST LIKE SO MANY PEOPLE IN THE WORLD TRULY ARE.
BUT, JEAN, WE ARE VERY MUCH THE SUM OF OUR PARTS...
AT THE SAME TIME, SOME OF US CAN BE SO MUCH MORE.
WHEN YOU LOST ANNIE IT OPENED A DOOR FOR YOU, AND YOU'VE STEPPED THROUGH IT INTO A WHOLE NEW WORLD.
WHETHER ANNIE HAD LIVED OR NOT, VERY LIKELY YOUR PATHS WOULD'VE DIVERGED.
YOUR POWERS WOULD'VE COME, AND YOU WOULD'VE TAKEN YOUR PLACE AT MY SIDE AS MY BEST PUPIL.
ANNIE WILL ALWAYS BE WITH YOU, JUST AS I WILL.

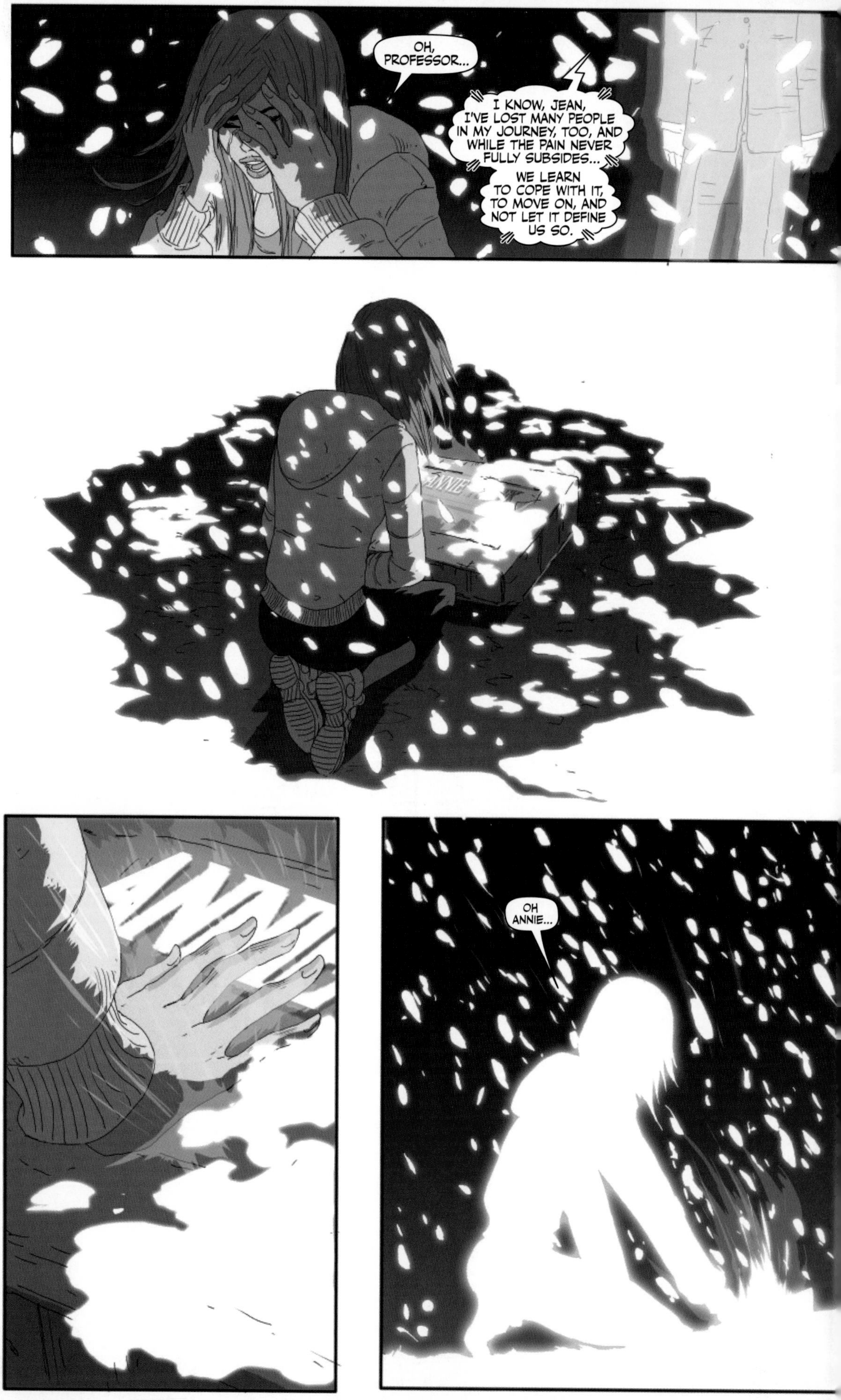
OH, PROFESSOR...
I KNOW, JEAN, I'VE LOST MANY PEOPLE IN MY JOURNEY, TOO, AND WHILE THE PAIN NEVER FULLY SUBSIDES...
WE LEARN TO COPE WITH IT, TO MOVE ON, AND NOT LET IT DEFINE US SO.
OH ANNIE...

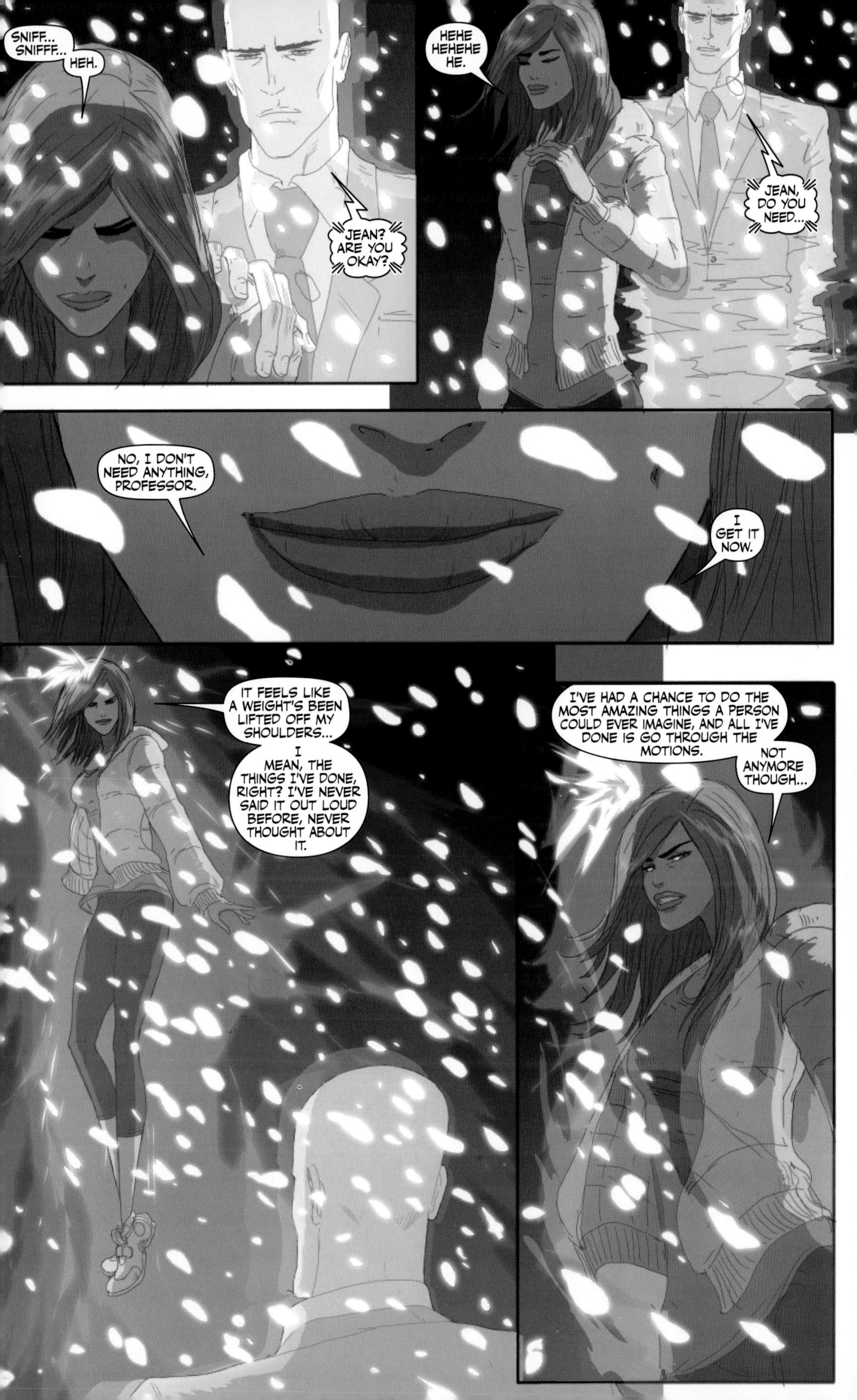
SNIFF... SNIFFF... HEH.
JEAN? ARE YOU OKAY?
HEHE HEHEHE HE.
JEAN, DO YOU NEED...
NO, I DON'T NEED ANYTHING, PROFESSOR.
I GET IT NOW.
IT FEELS LIKE A WEIGHT'S BEEN LIFTED OFF MY SHOULDERS...
I MEAN, THE THINGS I'VE DONE, RIGHT? I'VE NEVER SAID IT OUT LOUD BEFORE, NEVER THOUGHT ABOUT IT.
I'VE HAD A CHANCE TO DO THE MOST AMAZING THINGS A PERSON COULD EVER IMAGINE, AND ALL I'VE DONE IS GO THROUGH THE MOTIONS.
NOT ANYMORE THOUGH...

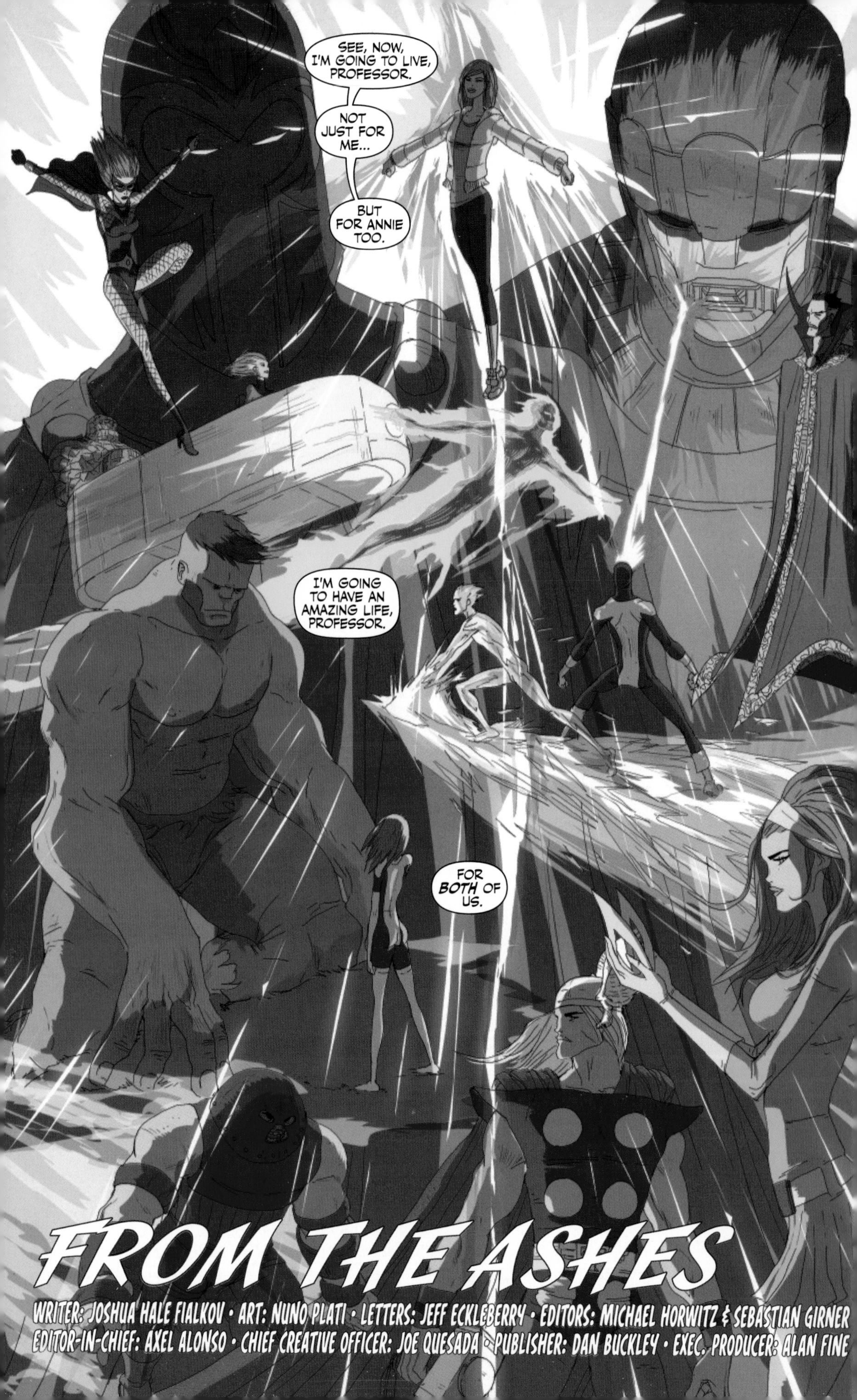
SEE, NOW, I'M GOING TO LIVE, PROFESSOR.
NOT JUST FOR ME...
BUT FOR ANNIE TOO.
I'M GOING TO HAVE AN AMAZING LIFE, PROFESSOR.
FOR *BOTH* OF US.
FROM THE ASHES
WRITER: JOSHUA HALE FIALKOV • ART: NUNO PLATI • LETTERS: JEFF ECKLEBERRY • EDITORS: MICHAEL HORWITZ & SEBASTIAN GIRNER
EDITOR-IN-CHIEF: AXEL ALONSO • CHIEF CREATIVE OFFICER: JOE QUESADA • PUBLISHER: DAN BUCKLEY • EXEC. PRODUCER: ALAN FINE